Spot's
Magical
Christmas

Eric Hill

It was Christmas Eve

and Spot was decorating the Christmas tree. It looked very pretty. He thought it would be perfect with a star on the top.

"I won't get Mum because she's busy wrapping presents. I'm sure I can reach if I just stretch up..."

Spot's mum, Sally, came in to see what the crash was.

"Spot, I think you're getting too excited about Christmas.
Why don't you go outside and help Dad collect some logs
for the fire?"

"All right, Mum," said Spot.
"I'll finish the tree later."

Spot put on his hat and scarf and rushed off to see his dad.

"Don't forget to shut the door, Spot," called Sally,
" – *quietly*."

But Spot had already closed the door with a nice loud bang
and didn't hear what she said.

Spot's dad, Sam, was loading logs into a basket. "Hello, Spot. I thought you were decorating the tree."

"I was, Dad, but the decorations were getting too excited."

Sam smiled. "Ah yes, they do that at this time of year."

And then a strange voice said, "Ahem. Excuse me. Hello." Spot and Sam looked all around. At first they couldn't see anyone, but then they realized that there was a head high up above the fence.

"Have you by any chance seen a sleigh?"

"A big red sleigh." A second head appeared over the fence.

"In fact, Santa's big red sleigh," said the two heads together. "He's going to need it tonight."

"Are you Santa's reindeer?" asked Spot.

"That's right. But we've lost Santa's sleigh. And if we don't find it there won't be any presents for anyone."

"But that's awful!" said Spot. "What are you going to do?"

"Keep on looking," said the reindeer gloomily. And they disappeared together into the woods.

Spot was very upset.

"You could help by asking your friends if they've seen the sleigh," suggested Sam.
"I'll try Helen first," said Spot.

Helen was in her kitchen making iced cookies. *"Cooee! Helen!"* shouted Spot. Helen jumped and the icing jumped.

"Helen, Santa's sleigh is lost and I'm helping to look for it. Have you seen it?"

"Is it big and red?"

"Yes, yes, it is."

"I thought it would be. No, I haven't seen it. But why don't you ask Tom? I'll come and help when I've finished these."

"Right," said Spot. "I'll take one of these cookies with me."

"They're not ready," said Helen. But Spot had gone.

Tom was putting up paper-chains when Spot suddenly rang the doorbell.
Tom jumped and the paper-chains jumped and wound themselves all round him.

"Tom, have you seen Santa's sleigh? It's lost and he needs it to deliver all the presents."

But Tom hadn't seen Santa's sleigh either. "Maybe Steve has seen it. You go and ask him and I'll help look in a little while."

"I think your decorations are getting too excited, Tom," said Spot.

"Steve, Steve, are you there?" called Spot, rattling the letter-box.
Steve was wrapping up a beautiful new ball which was his
Christmas present for Spot. He jumped and the ball jumped and
bounced all round the room. "Just a minute," shouted Steve,
and finally managed to chase the ball into a cupboard.
"Come in, Spot, the door isn't locked."

Spot explained about Santa's sleigh.
"I haven't seen a big red sleigh," said Steve. "But I *have*
seen a small blue sledge."
"Where?"
"Here. It's my own blue sledge.
Let's take it out for a ride."

"We ought to be looking for Santa's sleigh but... well, all right, perhaps we can search and ride at the same time."

Steve and Spot pushed the sledge up to the top of a long hill and climbed on.

"Hold tight, Spot!"

The sledge started to pick up speed. Helen and Tom appeared at the bottom of the hill.

"Look out, Helen! Look out, Tom!"

The sledge went hurtling down the hill and came to a sudden stop in a pile of soft snow.

"That was great, Steve. Let's do it again."

"We've been looking everywhere but we can't find Santa's sleigh," said Helen. "Have you seen it?"

"Just a minute," said Steve. "What's that among the trees?"

There was something red showing through the bushes.

"Great, you've found it!" said Tom.

"But that's not Santa's sleigh," said Spot.

"No, it's my ball," said Tom. "I lost it yesterday. What luck!"

"Can we go for a ride on the sledge now?" asked Helen.

"Of course," said Steve. "Don't be long."

"Keep looking for Santa's sleigh," said Spot.

Helen and Tom pulled Steve's sledge up the hill.

"Your sledge is really great," said Spot. "I wish I could have one like it."

"You should have put one on your list for Santa to bring," said Steve.

"It's too late," said Spot. "Anyway Santa won't be bringing *anything* this year if we don't find his sleigh."

Helen and Tom came whizzing down.

"Wheee, that was fun!" said Helen.

"We didn't see Santa's sleigh," said Tom.

"Now we'll just have one more ride," said Steve. "Let's go further down the hill."

"Jump on, you two," said Helen. "We'll give you a push."

"Ready, steady, *go!*" Tom and Helen pushed the sledge with all their might and it shot off down the slope, faster and faster, and didn't stop until it was right among the trees.

"Whoosh!" said Spot. "That was a long one. But Steve, *look there!*"

Steve turned to look. "Helen! Tom! Come and see what Spot has found!"

"It's very big," said Helen.
  "And very red," said Tom.
  "It really is Santa's sleigh," said Steve.

"Well," said Spot, "now we have to find the reindeer. I'll go and tell Dad."

"It's time we all went home," said Helen. "But your dad will know what to do."

"Good luck, Spot!" they shouted, as he ran off.

Sam was just finishing loading the logs.

"We found the sleigh, Dad. It's in the woods!"

"My goodness! Well done!"

"But how can I find the reindeer to tell them?"

"Follow their footprints, of course!"

Two lines of prints led clearly away through the snow. "This is easy," said Spot. He put his head down to the track and ran as fast as he could in and out of the trees, and round and round in circles until he was quite dizzy. Then suddenly, *bump!* – he stumbled right into some very long legs.

"I'm sorry, I'm looking for... Oh, I'm looking for *you!*"
"I think you've found us," said the reindeer.
"And I've found your sleigh as well."
"That's wonderful! Jump on and show us the way."

"This is even more fun than the sledge," said Spot.

"If you think this is fun," said the reindeer, "you should try the sleigh. Would you like to?"

"Oh *yes*," said Spot. "Look, we're passing my house now. Let me ask Dad."

Sam was doubtful at first. "It's getting very late, Spot."

"We won't be gone long," said the first deer.

"No time at all, really," said the second deer.

"All right, Spot, since it's Christmas," said Sam. "But you must come back before it gets dark."

"Thanks, Dad," said Spot.

The reindeer were delighted to find there wasn't
a scratch on the sleigh.
    "In you get, Spot, and let's go!"

The sleigh gathered speed as it came out
of the woods and skimmed over the
ground. Spot saw his house
with the Christmas tree
in the window.

Suddenly they were high in the sky
and Spot's house looked like a little toy.
He could see Tom's and Helen's and Steve's houses,
and the whole countryside spread out far below.
The sky darkened and lights went on
all over the village.

Then he looked up.
    "Oh, the stars!"
    "He likes stars," said
the first deer.
    "Then stars it is!"
said the other deer.
    The sleigh flew up into
the sky in a huge loop
and the stars fell
sparkling in a great trail
all around them.

"Mountains ahead!" called
the reindeer.
   "That's funny!" said Spot.
"There are no mountains
round here."
   But sure enough,
a vast range of mountains
loomed directly in front.

The sleigh seemed to slow down to go along a valley among the
mountains. At the end of the valley was a cave in the rock
and the sleigh flew right into the entrance of the cave.

Spot gasped in amazement. He had never seen so much bustle
and activity.

"Why, it's Santa's workshop!" he said. And at that moment Santa himself appeared from an opening in the rock wall and waved to Spot. Spot could hardly believe his eyes.

"Now it's time we got you home," said the reindeer. "We've a busy night ahead."

The sleigh left the cave and the mountains and flew back
through the stars down to Spot's village,
and finally came to land beside Spot's house.

"Oh, thank you," said Spot. "That was like... like magic!"

"Well, Christmas is magical," said the reindeer.

Spot looked up at the sky. It was still daylight and he couldn't see the stars.

When he turned round, the reindeer and sleigh had disappeared.

Sam was still standing by the pile of logs exactly where Spot had left him. "Hello, Spot, I thought you were going for a ride."

"Yes, I've been, Dad. It was wonderful."

"That didn't take long," said Sam.

"No, no time at all, really," said Spot.

Spot went indoors and told his mum all about his exciting adventure.

She pulled a large Christmas stocking out of a drawer. "I think you need to hang this up, Spot. Santa will be here soon."

Spot looked out of the window. Now it was dark.

"Yes, I know, Mum," he said.

And just for a moment, high above among the stars, he saw the two reindeer and Santa in the big red sleigh.

And in the morning there was one very special extra present waiting for Spot...

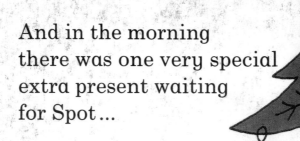

To Spot from